Dear parents,

Math anxiety. So many of us su Yet every day we measure time or distance, look for patterns, estimate, and count. Whether we realize it or not, we are constantly thinking mathematically. And as parents we hope that our children will not succumb to our math prejudices.

We give children a great deal of encouragement when they are learning to count—but the encouragement needn't stop there. Young children love puzzles and riddles, and they eagerly approach problem-solving situations as if they were games. They often see and use a variety of strategies. These are important skills in developing mathematical thinking.

We truly have the power to nurture in our children a long-lasting love for math. We can do this by making a "math connection" to familiar experiences and by supporting our children's natural affinity for the discipline. **Step into Reading® + Math** books can help. Each book combines an age-appropriate math element with an enjoyable reading experience.

Remember—math is not an isolated phenomenon but is woven into the fabric of our lives. The love of math is a lifelong journey. Celebrate that journey with your child!

Colleen DeFoyd
Primary grades math teacher
Scottsdale, Arizona

To my boys, Mike and Alexander
—J.G.

To Makenna
—M.W.

Text copyright © 2000 by Dr. Julie Glass.
Illustrations copyright © 2000 by Mike Wohnoutka.
All rights reserved under International and Pan-American Copyright Conventions.
Published in the United States by Random House, Inc., New York, and simultaneously
in Canada by Random House of Canada Limited, Toronto.

www.randomhouse.com/kids

Library of Congress Cataloging-in-Publication Data
Glass, Julie.
Counting Sheep / by Julie Glass ; illustrated by Mike Wohnoutka.
    p.   cm. — (Step into reading + math. A step 1 book)
SUMMARY: A child counts sheep and other animals in multiples of two, three, four, and
five before falling asleep.
ISBN 0-375-80619-9 (trade) — ISBN 0-375-90619-3 (lib. bdg.)
[1. Bedtime—Fiction.   2. Sleep—Fiction. 3. Animals—Fiction.   4. Counting.
5. Multiplication—Fiction.]
I. Wohnoutka, Mike, ill. II. Title. III. Step into reading + math. Step 1 book.
PZ7.G481235 Co 2000 [E]—dc21 00-025695

Printed in the United States of America October 2000 10 9 8 7 6 5 4 3 2 1

Step into Reading® + Math

Counting Sheep

T 23270

By Dr. Julie Glass

Illustrated by Mike Wohnoutka

A Step 1 Book

Random House 🏠 New York

I cannot sleep.

So I count sheep.

Here they come.

One by one.

One, then two,
three, four, and five.
They jump.
They leap.
And some skydive!

Look!
Something new—
a kangaroo!

More hop in.
Two by two.

Two, four, six,
and eight, and ten.
This one wants
to be my friend!

Now funny monkeys
visit me.
They come in.
Three by three.

Some small.

Some tall.

Some in between.

Three, six, nine,

twelve, and fifteen.

Now what do I see?

It is a bee!

Here are some more.

Four by four.

Four, and eight,

twelve, sixteen, twenty.

Twenty is plenty!

Five sheep,
ten kangaroos,
fifteen monkeys,
twenty bees.

Oh, no!
Go away, bees!
Please!

24

Away go the monkeys.

Three by three.

Fifteen, twelve, nine,

six, three, zero.

Away go the kangaroos.
Two by two.
Ten, eight, six,
four, two, zero.

Away go the sheep.
One by one.
Five, four, three,
two, one, zero.

Zero monkeys.

Zero kangaroos.

Zero sheep.

Zero bees...

...ZZZZZZZZZZ